LIFE MOVES OUTSIDE

© 1987 by Barbara Einzig

Some of these works first appeared in Bachy, Credences, El Velamen, How(ever), In'hui, Invisible City, Island, Magazine, Multiples, O.ARS, Pig Iron, Ploughshares, Snap, Temblor, Writing *and* Zero.

This project is in part supported by grants from the Rhode Island State Council on the Arts and the Rhode Island Foundation, a charitable community trust serving the people of Rhode Island.

Library of Congress Cataloging in Publication Data
Einzig, Barbara, 1951—
   Life moves outside
   I. Title
PS3555.I6L5 1987   813'.54   85-46052
ISBN 0-930901-42-8 (pbk.)

BARBARA EINZIG

Life Moves Outside

BURNING DECK
Providence

CONTENTS:

Reading for Pleasure	9
George, the Name of a Fish	11
Where We Are	15
Three for Jeremy	22
Seeking Understanding	24
Composition in an Even Tone	25
For November's Clear Sun	35
What Follows Evening	37
The Slide Show	39
"The World of Action is a World of Stones"	42
"Within Herself Each Part Was Free, Although It Did What Was Expected"	44
Life Moves Outside	49

I wrote with every sailing and spent a little fortune on cables, but there was no reply.

—Emma Goldman

The book is the place of the neutral whose aloofness is always in danger.

—Edmond Jabès

Reading for Pleasure

HE WROTE THAT the light struck the window blind and he should have stopped there, as he had stopped to see it, struck, the light, the glass. These things are repeated forever and we attempt to read and understand them, the way one reads a poem, and one stops in the reading over and over while going on.

Searching behind the pronoun in the dark looking with the hands for a false wall. This is who I am. Don't take it personally. How can I help it. This kind of poetry she criticizes as a form of packaging, but we want to open our eyes.

The ocean he said is humiliating in its disguises. Encantados are pure spirit, they have no shadows. A sentence certainly looks forward and backward and that makes a darkness around its line, nimbus. These are buildings that make things happen inside or outside, and all people open windows as far as I know.

They brought up the child in the usual way, but without a name. Others struggled to name him in order to call him, but to no avail, they only let out a sound which struck the back of his steadily larger head, the way it would hit a lamp post. When he got to an age when he was open to discussing personal matters with some trace of objectivity, he was firmly persuaded a name was a necessary aspect of being human, and at this time he took on the name Norman, though it never seemed to fit him.

The feathers of the birds are red or orange or blue or green, colors unknown to a bird or as words to viewers in a foreign climate. The words just pour out like water, splashing or being absorbed into the ground. Do you consider writing a form of self-expression, either in the formation of the letters themselves, as in calligraphy, or in what thoughts or meanderings these characters compose?

George, the Name of a Fish

WHAT SHE WAS RESISTING in him, or in his habits, or in his world of clothing and cars and books, she could not say. It was just important to not make what it was her own, and the only way to do that was resistance, an energy employed in constant tiny, invisible ways, with the aptitude of hemming, but with confusion in the garment or body of their love.

Sentences became longer and more explanatory, their conversation more and more a proof in search of some theorem, their reason for or in being together. Finally she went along with some small part of what she had instinctively been against.

All of these things are trivial, domestic dioramas or shrines which only coinhabitants of a house may visit, or find. (Trivia was the goddess, he said, of the three roads, their meeting.)

One day the light of mid-afternoon, of mid-winter in a warm climate, filled the room as water does an aquarium. Here is the fish, suggesting what is necessary to take care of it.

It was his fish, he had bought it, having always wanted to have one, having always wanted to buy one. It was a Japanese fighting fish, and its exotic and vicious quality rendered innocent through isolation drew him to it.

She saw the green algae growing thick in the round, clear, moonlike container and purchased a snail, having read that they delight in consuming that very problem. The snail first sat on the bottom, on green gravel, but then began inching its way upward, and she saw the softness of its body through the glass, what was normally inside the shell.

Soon there was more than one snail, though tiny there were many, and the algae only partially cleared

GEORGE, THE NAME OF A FISH

to reveal their small growing bodies among the green gravel, the color and softness of their young shells nearly identical to the adult body she had observed adhering to the glass.

If the world of the fish was his, he should be the one to clean it, and so she left this scene to develop, but occasionally she was so bold as to look at the fish, and the sight was disturbing. There he swam, but his activity lessened more and more each day, the fish dwelt closer to the bottom of the aquarium, site of the snail's origin, the warrior's kimono of primary colors fading with a declension identical to that of his swimming.

Finally she cleaned this out (this was her giving in), scooping and rescuing the fish in a cup designed for drinking coffee, and put him in a beautifully empty (except for water) bowl, being careful to first add a few drops of a liquid resembling water in appearance, but thicker, that makes tap water safe for fish.

The day the light looked that way what was in the jar she dumped into a colander normally used to wash spaghetti or lettuce, and the snails, unable to express their disgruntlement at the fall, were dumb there with the pea gravel. She threw all of them out but one, and then, after scrubbing the aquarium free of scum till it shone in the yellow sun brilliant in the kitchen, she returned the clean gravel, inserted a new plant purchased for the occasion, and added the fish, tipped slowly from its bowl, and more water.

She did other things too that let the resistance go, a rein, new things that were larger she went along with until suddenly this amounts to submission.

All the energy previously employed in the invisible hemming, in the resistance to this submission, was then returned, an unearned gift miraculous as her own life, to her, she who walks out the door as she has so many times before but without this time returning.

Where we are

THE CHILDREN in the game were asked what it was to be a mystery, and they answered individually and impatiently, in short phrases, many from television. They used the words "robber," "to find where something is lost," "if something is stolen," "if the detective looked for someone dead," etc.

The small boy moved quickly, shifting his weight from one foot to the other in a stable, light fashion, as if punctuating feverishly. The girl was solemn and always seemed to be thinking. Her name was Noach; she had grey eyes and red hair, cut sharply at the neckline, so she appeared to have a cap on, and thinned bluntly just above the ear, creating a difference in color where the second stage began, two shades of orange, resembling the feathers of a bird.

As they are guided primarily by the constellations, they often become disoriented on foggy or overcast nights and frequently collide with such brightly colored objects as bridges, high-rise buildings, lighthouses, and radio and television towers. On such occasions the birds appear to be badly confused and even fly directly down into the ground.

A sentence makes its own speech. She makes her own bed, and lies in it. She rises upward of her own accord. She has changed her mind about how she feels about religion and the family, two categories which are often put together.

It is not necessary to be afraid. Come with me. That is a long hallway, and you are likely to get lost. Each one exists independently, and that is how they are moving, there is a stillness about each one while moving, as if the sound has been turned down, such that their movement has gravity. I like to look at the cars at the intersections this way. The green, yellow, and then red lights have a solemnity when seen from this perspective of silence.

It is this perspective which is employed in propaganda against nuclear war: it is mentioned that shadows are made permanent, that something flickers, the quality of abstraction that so empowers and afflicts our minds being momentarily realized physically.

Airport ceilometers, which measure the altitude of the cloud cover by shining a powerful searchlight vertically, often attract hundreds of birds which then may plunge to their deaths down the lethal light beam.

Her mother unexpectedly had told her that it was really mathematics that gave her the most pleasure, because if one slowed down and pored over it, all could be ordered there and certain. If one only slowed down and pored over it, all could be ordered there and certain.

The room is blue. In the morning light, pink, glows violet, small slice of cheese. Faintness, reticence.

The room is red. There is a bed. There is a bed with white sheets and people are in the room.

The moonlight shines in the window, falling on the wall. There is something lonely in walking through the dark room against, or under, or in, the moonlight which falls in stripes on the wall, made by venetian blinds, the old kind.

The moon was nearly full, and looked imperfect, as though dented. A piece of music hesitates and repeatedly falters when coming upon a scratch in its recording. Synthetic nature. Sympathetic nature. Psychic, she explained to him, is how you say it in English. It was calculated for a certain effect. They have forgotten how to speak and write. They have forgotten how to move and walk. They have forgotten what house they were originally living in.

They live as they did in their first country. They try to remember and to forget simultaneously, so as to adapt while feeling at home in memory. Forty-five is a strange age at which to be born. I came from there. I knew her there. You should have seen her there.

When you are finished with your tea there you turn over your cup and you take your remaining sugar, a piece, a small piece, and you put it on the bottom of the cup. Sugar was rare; this signifies taste.

True customs can never be truly old. To be old something must be felt as having in it something of another time, and a custom makes its own time, that is why it is a custom.

It begins with a few details of the doctor's possessions. We know nothing more than what we might have observed had we been there. The character of the doctor is convincing, told as a complicated gossip. She also is presented to us with the details of her circumstances, her surroundings. The feelings she falls into arise just as naturally, and we are forced to accept them in the same way we accept material reality. We do not know why these things are happening, and the way personal events fall into the doctor's musings on philosophy, etc., make us feel how intellectual strategies function in the same way as do fondnesses for particular colors of clothing.

Sunglasses, black and red, "wrap-around" kind, mask of a raccoon, those masks we wore at Halloween, they were cheap. Some were brittle plastic and those broke but some were felt, soft over the eyes. Black, pink, red, orange or silver, some had things attached to them, decorations.

The chaos of thoughts coheres in what is out the window. Pale half moon in a new sky. The sky is new in time though blue for in it is the moon. The moon always in the sky is now visible within it. Sometimes it is like chalk, like a disk. Just now the sun is at the exact moment, a station, where it turns from a flat form to an object which shines into the daylight. Then finally the sensation of daylight leaves, being absorbed into, becoming, the world.

In the morning I put on the record and let the waves of her voice exist. The sky is deepest blue (with cirrus clouds) on top, where we put it as children, and down below, in the white space where usually there were houses, there they are, with a white, slightly industrial light evenly shining up from behind them.

Now you know it is morning, with the light in the east, where I'm facing, and the palm trees still dark to all appearances. The sounds of birds are covered over by her voice.

With the power of a freeway being laid down in a dream over the vast South American rainforest, she experienced the desire to obliterate her past and, in that same impulse, driving an infinite hammer into memory, the horror of this negative construction. Its taste was the taste of poison. First they cleared everyone from the city. Three million people were obliged to leave in order for the perfect society to be built. Pieces of typewriters and telephones, obviously forcibly smashed and broken, can be seen.

Lassitude of crevices. A desire to forget. The rivers of forgetfulness and death. Those who forgot their real identity forgot their bodies which they had left in the other world and did not return for them. They remained forever the sloth's prisoners, dreaming.

One was the dream of the other, and so neither could really be killed without killing the other. The attempt to poison the past and litter it with her present body would eliminate a future which, even in its eliminated form, would then also be a double image of the poisoned past.

The woman on the radio advised the Israeli woman whose father had shaved her head in the middle of the night because he saw, through the curtains, the silhouette of her and her date kissing, had tried to shave her head and then she left the next day and five years later she married an Iranian but the story went on and on, it was a burdensome story she could barely get out from under, and there was a masterfulness in the pacing of this her story, because of its weighing on her mind, so that the story was not a recounting but an impression the story had left upon her with all its weight, it left a pattern on her mind, and the woman on the radio, the psychological popular advisor, advised this woman to make up her mind if she was going to live for her parents in which case divorce the non-Jewish husband or if she at thirty-six could choose to be her own woman and if so said the radio lady, stand up for what you want.

Three for Jeremy

1 THE AIR OF THE HOUSE of the past is light music on the skin, satin or a hand. Lists of the house's furniture break our movement, silently, comma, the collapse. Animal falls in twilight film, maybe a horse. Extensive documentation in the other world proved intention; but right now our presence, yours and mine, in the dream of the house of the past is (verb) solid as a lake.

Blue or alpine, no words or names appended to anything, not even the distance of grammar in our relation.

2

I LOOKED to those mirrors also, dictating the reflection of my glance. Waking to write again after a long time, the bell rings. There must be a circus outside, or a church. The windows are open, and there are the rings where the children are striving, at recess, as she said. As she wrote, waking in the night, or the memory of tetherball, and all mixed time. There are marbles in the garden, orange, blue, veined, round, four of them. They sing. Babies should be careful not to swallow them, but they can sit in the chairs made for jumping without moving from their places, only up and down, on which a thin bar is positioned in front, like a piano, at which the baby plays, in primary colors, blue, red, and yellow. Fingers flick the balls and the paint wears in that way, way of the first thought, and the second ones.

3

OARS AND THE SMALL LIFEBOAT, and the expanse of sea, the time of swimming, measured by a clock in a pool. All things glow underwater and though the sense of sight is distorted, one's wet skin finds new sense in its motion through the waves. This is the ocean, this rhyme, that eel moving its graygreen head, wise, thin, sinuous prince. So old, a turtle, the hood and the retreat. This is all under water where other fish go, breathing in some way I can't understand, and my own suspended, leaf in air.

Seeking Understanding

WEEDING'S SINCERE, grinning's a game. When I touch you with my hand, please kiss me on my face. Not there. On the lips a smile.

Furrow or row, a name. When my eyes fall on yours, they are suspended. Give directions clearly. Bend down.

The weeds advance in clusters, lettuce seeds itself. When the heat brings on these changes, observing the environment, new plantings are made and the old ones pulled up.

But not by the roots, which serve to aerate the topsoil so that the new roots, also blind, may find more open space in which to spread their wings. The insect falls.

Like my eyes? I do. I'm not sure what you use this fruit for. Help me out with it, you're from around here.

Sure I am, but I've never seen anything resembling that. What did you say your name was?

Composition in an Even Tone

AS I BEGIN to write this, my husband comes into the room. He will undoubtedly speak to me now, when I don't want him to, even though he has himself been sitting, for the past half-hour of my pacing, in an armchair in the living room, reading the newspaper.

I move about, longing for conversation, although I have nothing to say to him. I consult the dictionary, change the water of the flowers, and try to think about my daughter's arrival tomorrow. But these activities are disturbed by my husband's presence. He always seems to promise something, turning the pages.

That's what I did then, moved and stopped and moved again, all the while waiting for this thing he promises, but then I turned on my heel, passed through the hall, entered the dining room, and sat

> down at the table where I now write, surely with no less self-absorption than he had in the living room, reading in his chair.

The migration of swifts in the spring: in the air they feed, gather stuff for their nests and even copulate while flying from their winter home in Africa over all the western European nations until they reach the space of the sky above the slats of our fence, but I have never seen them set down there, and through my glasses their legs appear to be small and weak.

> Of course the newspaper is a large thing spread out, a thin sheet held between the hands, that makes noise. Even people who regularly begin and finish things skim it. My husband usually reads the beginnings of three or four "big" stories on the front page, the news, and then turns it, looking over the second and third page with a wide, diagonal glance from page three to page two, as if drawing a light smeary line with his eye from right to left. Some ads catch his attention; in the center of page two the condensed news in little blocks next to bullets gets stared at momentarily, as if remembering something.

> He'll read something there, anything he feels like, just enough of the story to find out what it's about.
>
> Then his arms, holding the paper open, begin to feel heavy and awkward, as they do when hanging up a large load of clothes, and he turns to a long story, usually in the business section, almost always one about an immediate problem of some big company, and what they said yesterday they'll be doing about it today or this week.
>
> To someone coming to the door it might look like my husband was doing almost nothing, that promising quality, just looking at the paper in an interruptable sort of way, but to a person familiar with this reading, such as myself, his action is one of a discipline made no more approachable by its being a habit.

As long as he had been around he had been a kind of metronome for her. This is why, she explains as she once again takes up the study of the piano, she lacks an internal sense of timing.

Listening to her younger sister typing for her father in the summer she explained that speed would always be elusive unless one learned to hit each key with equal force.

Over the years she had observed that almost anyone could come knocking at the door but everyone felt obliged to attempt to introduce themselves and, with a few memorable exceptions, did not enter uninvited.

Called limpiacasa *because it often enters suburban houses and forages in the rooms for spiders and insects.*

> The grass is green, too long, almost bending over in this wind that's just started, because my sister and her family were here this week from back east and I didn't have time to mow it.
>
> Two months ago the gardener got sick, and I keep thinking he's going to get better, so I haven't looked for anyone new yet.
>
> The zinnias in the border had become stiff and dry-looking, so I pulled them all out and put in a lot of pieces of our neighbor's chrysanthemum, the yellow one, to root and fill in there. Through the slats of the fence I can see the meadow, if that's what you call it, a big wild space that at this time of year has seeds blowing all over the place.

Terrestrial algae, fungi, mosses and ferns all produce fine dustlike spores, allowing them to travel all over the globe. In fact, there are always spores of these plants present in the air. This is why when making jam it is so essential to seal the jars right away.

> The development of open space has been a source of conflict for over four years, and when you walk over there and follow those streams — where you can still almost get lost — it's hard not to think of the court battles.

Tornadoes and whirlwinds may suck potential cuttings high into the air and carry them over great distances.

Intimate knowledge of familiar areas.

Falling on the bed right into it, heavy, inert, working long hours she fell asleep fast. Waking to the alarm she was up immediately, and so what had gone on in between was so private as to be hidden even from her. She preferred to get up long before going to work, so she would have some time to herself to think. When she did not she became a sort of sponge, full of the tasks assigned to her. The sponge worked all day, wringing out, wiping up. It came

home, fed itself, straightened a little (adhering to
an aesthetic developed in a former era of consciousness), read until falling asleep with the lights
on, usually no more than one page.

Looking at the pictures of themselves at all ages,
they encountered themselves as they would other
people. After seeing many slides of former instants,
one failed to identify with the more distant shots.
He thought of the word "turnover" and all that it
implied, and wondered, if his own had been so
total, what could be said to now be the same.

His head bowed itself down slightly so as to examine
his hands with his eyes. His body itself was bewildered with itself, his head was made up of some
stuff, carried, a fire or intelligence, a mess he couldn't
see whose order and thought was present and
persistent but, for that moment, not his own. He
heard his wife later telling a neighbor in a worried
voice that he had lately been acting "a little disoriented." He felt a sharp anger whose sensation
matched that of the pains he had been experiencing,
and as he knew this it too detached itself from him
and moved away from him, not his own.

> Maybe my daughter Alex and I will walk
> over there tomorrow, if it doesn't rain.
> The rains have started early this year.
> The first are usually a drizzle, like a fog

but coming down from above, out of a denser whiteness. People stay inside but I go out. The air is soft, a barrier that moves as I step forward, turning down the streets where I know that gardens of ferns and impatiens are flourishing, flowers reduced to their color in the thick wetness.

But all that, like my pacing about, was in another time, and this year there were no preliminaries. A storm fell out of a sky that earlier that day had been one of summer — sun, heat, sprinklers, around them children in sunsuits, weaving in and out of bright water, yelling.

Plants, in the same way as animals, are adapted for movement, but instead of legs and fins they have adaptations, such as wings and floats, to carry them away from their parents, enabling them to reach a new site and establish a separate existence.

"Mother," I said, "mother, mother." And as I knew she wasn't there, the word formed a new shape in the air. She didn't answer to it, it didn't attach itself to her, she didn't, she couldn't take it in. That's what they say about colors too, the sky is blue because red and yellow get absorbed but the blue rays scatter.

> Alex was not always Alex. I named her Alicia, after someone I'd known in high school — not very well, but I always liked and admired her.

She was notorious in her constant watching of her children, of every move they made. Unconscious of invading their privacy, she experienced her own curiosity and aggression as a mounting uneasiness or hunger inside of her. As this increased she not only glanced sideways but stared at them, asking many questions. To have something of themselves left they retreated into themselves, and she felt without knowing why a desperation and would "accidentally" come across pieces of paper, photographs, plans, signs of lives they possessed and were keeping from her.

No one ever saw it court, copulate, or lay and brood eggs, so it was assumed to have a fabulous origin.

In turn when her children were grown and she was finally gone, rather than feeling free they were like people so used to a disturbing noise they cannot sleep without it. They were not used to feeling any space about themselves. With the withdrawal of her gaze they were as if thrown into a new element, exposed. Furthermore their retreat into themselves, now that it was no longer a defense from a present threat, came into its own as a vacancy, a lack of connection with others. And this they began to fill by going after people in the same way, getting close to them, not letting them move.

The home range of a house sparrow, Passer domesticus, may be no more than the size of two domestic gardens.

My immediate neighbors choose the lottery animals on the basis of dreams and clouds. They dream of someone and ask that person which animal they identify with, and then they choose that one. Me, I'm a monkey. She's a deer. They don't have them here but she saw one in a book and read they are quiet and fast. So when I dream of her I just choose giraffe, think of her that way, because the woman who sings sells giraffes. I already know this so I don't have to ask. Or maybe they look up and right away see an animal, an elephant in the sky, its trunk and wrinkled feet. That's how it works, but I'm not lucky, my wife says the animals hide from me.

Grazing. In Scotland the red deer live up high and lower down too, like in the song. At the beginning of summer the mothers have their does lower down and the males come downhill too to mate with them in the autumn. When it's bad weather they come down too. The deer move up during the day and come part way down at night, so it depends, and they go uphill a little at a time in the spring. But that's all I know, because my sister wrote that to me in a letter.

My daughter changed it from Alicia to Alex when she was ten, because she said she didn't like the sound of it.

Solitary, perches hidden in the lower and middle branches, feeds on birds and lizards which it captures by chasing through dense vegetation. Attracted to birds following army ants. Call: a series of barking sounds like that of a small dog.

Alex was always a stubborn person, but now she is less so. Things change. When she and her brother were here the house seemed too small, but now it's been almost five years since I've seen her. She's been living in East Africa, studying the movement of the elephants up and down Mount Kenya. She and her brother keep telling me to travel, and so does my husband, who has to go on a lot of trips. But I don't see any reason to — he's going on business and there's nothing for me to do there. And if I want to go sightseeing or look at things, there are plenty of things to look at around here.

For November's Clear Sun

GOING OFF INTO the sun layers of clothing are removed. Strike two. Seeing is believing I declare. Let us go together. Do you remember when we learned to read. That sentence is not a true question, it does not rise at the end but is flat, as a kite in slight wind, tied to something known, calm. Our hands, learning to turn white pages without tearing. For I think I know what it was like: that makes a hardwood stage, a statement, to feel that way about it. Come sit here in my living room chair.

The bat swings hits the ball the boy who hit it lets the bat go out of his hands the bat flies back as the ball flies. And is caught. While he is running. He does not fly.

Going off into the sun I was wearing wax, a suit my father made me, wings. The myth I remember in time for the sun. Yellow sun. Strike one. For it is warm here so skin is uncovered. The dog throws himself repeatedly against the fence, crazed with secret purpose. He is already out of the picture. I can break this movement or object. Again I dictate the reflection of my glance, for writing is a mirror, a target whose eye is a pool.

We went wading and there are polliwogs. The mud is thick on toes and it smells like summer. But now, here, it smells like fall, for it is November. The home plate is gone; the diamond is not being used — chalk is worn, blurred. I remember part of it — a vacancy taken up.

What Follows Evening

NIGHT SUSPENDS COLOR in its turning away, in its bringing up of whiteness in darkness. Daisies are iridescent in moonlight. This heightening is not rising of blood or an expression to a face. This is the way dream people become sensible.

Sleep suspends a daytime body, giving the weightless weight, by stealing from a daytime body its daytime gravity. This is not the enlivening of ghosts. A shadow moves this way with a hand over paper, with a body over pavement. This is a dream house with clear wide windows. If these windows are opened, they open into bright day. A dreamer becomes a sensation of falling, and having entered day by mistake, awakes suddenly.

Now I remember the Memling portraits — face of a woman or a man close up, study in steady character occurring as a flower in the face — and, framed by a window without glass, in a space equal, or existing equally through proportion, fields roads hills beyond. This is not a memory going backwards. This is a painting you may or may not know.

Night paints the face of a dreamer the way a loved one sleeping looks. Night turns away from that which the sleeper turns, as she turns her head on a pillow. This is the way dream people become sensible. In busy streets, noticing, they brush past each other, and may or may not recognize each other. A dreamer becomes a sensation of falling, and having entered day by accident, awakes suddenly. In one stroke, spell or die is cast and broken. This is a painting you may or may not know.

The Slide Show

SLOWLY THINGS get rich, as if underwater, forms multiply in the grace of color. Steel blue with black stripes, fish swim in water imaginary as the past. What is made up is the coral reef, with its symbiosis and clown fish hiding like words. In the turtle's eight-foot-long body, in its gigantic swimming, comparisons vanish and turn to silence.

Maybe something is orange here, something may be poisonous, the stone fish in its generous shape disappears. Red fish match the underside of coral.

I saw these small fish once before in dust swimming in sunlight slowly things were poor in air and moved without halting. I drew in the air and it was clean or dirty; I stood in the sun yellow and streaming or behind a cloud. I stand back and I look out the window; my face is hidden in the darkness you see.

People who view me as another species are living around me. Others come to me looking for the truth. Slowly culture disappears into the culture of a photograph, into a voice without location. On the ground my feet complain and suffer.

Danger is a relative matter terribly linked with knowledge. My eyesight isn't what it used to be. The sentences are each letters mailed from different countries, arriving to tell their stories after they have occurred.

Despite their impoverishment, nevertheless they bear witness. By repeating what they are saying over and over, though incomprehensible, the nature of what they have endured becomes clear.

Some have cut vast stones out of the faces of mountains; the hair of some turns red from malnutrition. These things are recorded fairly simply — in their own images, if with imperfect exposure. The things I say end with their own breath; they vanish and turn to silence; their repetitions now falter evenly as the steps of very old people do when they walk.

THE SLIDE SHOW 41

My age is the age I live in. My costume mimics another era.

The spell here is made out of its breaking, out of the startling rise of a school. I could have made you happier by telling you a story of someone who left for work and came home to dinner. But some of those who left for work have disappeared, but all of those who leave for work disappear. Made out of my own language, flayed, transported, forgiven. The messages I find in weather are eternal. Everyone in the village wears the same hat.

Imagine that, a city grown over, four generations of Incas living in an unknown spot. I see a face in the coral and you do also. The windows are without glass, wooden they open inward. You turn your memory into my voice and I turn my memory in yours, gigantic swimming of our relation. The air I drew in turns into an outward breath, word or song. They are surrounded by solids, fluids and gases. They are surrounded by things they cannot see that they understand through their minds, that they hold in mind.

Imagine that, a language grown over, once people lived there, once people lived inside those structures we see from above, on the wall as colored light.

"The world of action
is a world of stones"

(William Carlos Williams)

I MIXED A PERSONAL and an impersonal pronoun. I was part of that sensation. I belonged to another club, that travelled without speaking. I had become so very tired that I was almost without identity. Yet I did become irritable, and was known as a person it was best to stay away from. Nevertheless, I remained interested in the details of my dress. Nothing so complex as the triangular folding of handkerchiefs, and the way pockets display them, but basic colors, and whether my skirt was full or straight. I discovered my voice to be that of someone coquettish, kittenish, but too old for this role. So I would turn it upon children without warning, and they never responded well to me. We were walking through a largely magic garden. I saw him not as a rich man nor as my husband's employer but as someone who through being there made me notice all the flowers, one by one. First I saw a big rose, such as appear in cut glass in houses, or in old pickle jars, or in vases large enough for only one stem. Then another kind of rose, smaller, wilder. Then lilies. Of course I knew that none of this was "natural." It was a cultivated garden. Still, I had never looked at them before. I suppose in this sense it would be right to consider me dumb. What, then, did I look at before? Exactly, I was preoccupied with myself. And why? Because I was concerned with attracting the one I was with. But this man was a blind sort of man, a prophet or an enemy, someone who could never seem familiar. I tried to imagine him in a grocery store but knew he would enter there without being there, and thus would emerge unclaimed, unscathed. And because this man was blind, I lost this preoccupation with myself. I could not endeavor to attract a man who did not (through his eyes) notice things. And so I began to notice them, as if to make up for it. A case of the blind leading the blind, as the adage goes. Who knows these things anymore? And I cried, out, in the wilderness, but my cry did not come back to me. It rang as the sound of another person. It carried and mixed with sounds of other people. They lived in houses whose walls form the line of the street, broken by small entrances. With my cry he waved his hand toward a distance, as if tracing his own gesture. He did this often with sounds of uncertain origin. I am not exactly sorry. Certainly it seems that my life would have been less complicated, had I resisted my desire.

"Within herself each part
was free, although it did what was expected"

(Rose Drachler)

IT HAPPENED ONE DAY that he was walking into town by the old road and saw a woman up ahead, sitting by a stall. She did not look like the women usually there; maybe it was the way she was sitting that made her chair so separate, as if she herself were not selling oranges and avocados but only sitting next to them, watching the stand for someone else who could not be present but had a proprietary interest.

The way she was sitting, in profile to his approach, made her chair so separate from the landscape she floated, that way, into his view and attention.

He wasn't the kind of man who was out looking for a woman or for anything, but he had a good eye, and knew something when he saw it.

Later after he had married her she was walking next to him and looking up at something he would have said was in front of her, but the sky being so big there, nothing but fields all around, he had to just say it was in the air. She was walking next to him and looking up at something in the air. He didn't see what it was, just noticing her blue eyes and their smooth, slow movement upward, opening wider as they saw. He thought back and could not remember if she had been wearing a hat that day by the roadstand.

The chair separated itself from the dark dusty pavement, the wooden stall, and the apricot trees in full fruit, entering the remembered view as a white, horizontal thing, high and carried, resembling a hat.

He had loaned his car, a new Mercury, to his brother to go to the show. He hadn't really needed anything in town but decided to check and see if a part he had ordered had come in. Since the new highway had gone through the old road was better for walking and at the right time of year (and there were several, this being California) where one used to drive through blooming orange groves, closing the eyes, wind and speed a penetration into fragrance, one could now walk, and walking spread the sweetness out and around one. Some trees were stronger than others and walking it was not dangerous to close one's eyes and apprehend them one by one, as if it were a garden.

Once the traffic was diverted the commercial center shifted and the town stopped being a place with a road running through it and became a town by the side of the road on the way to Los Angeles from San Diego. As he remarked on this change to himself he remembered something his father had told him. Years ago the streets had Spanish names and someone was hired to choose new English ones. All the signs came down and people kept calling streets by their old names but then this became an old habit, and later knowing the old names was an indication of being old, and their regular use a sign of a conservative and then resistant nature, and later people who did not know any of this had ever happened thought him a little senile.

And it was true that much later he could not say for sure if this was the way he met his wife or if he had seen her there first, in that blue sundress, but had met her later, at a movie or at the home of a friend. Sometimes like a shadow above his head it fell into his thinking that this woman in the blue dress had been another woman entirely and not his wife at all, but this shadow made such a big darkness there that the stranger immediately became his wife, through and through, inside in who she had turned out to be, and outside in her skin, the folds and tensions of the blue cloth draped over her body as a dress, the outline of her as he first saw her from far away in profile in front of him in the air.

"WITHIN HERSELF..."

His young son with a new scissors got himself into trouble for cutting his mother carefully out of pictures and hiding her in magazines, which on questioning he could neither identify nor find, or setting her with bits of tape curled up to make a sticker of her, into another spot in the same photograph.

He had never seen her there before, and she did not look like the women usually minding those places by the road. Those other women looked like everything else there. They blended in with the dust and fruit and passing cars. Everything baked together in the sun.

She was looking down at her hands but he could not say if she had been occupied in any task such as patching or embroidery. She was looking down at her hands as if they were a part of her dress. Next to her a rope of garlic was hanging (they were close to Mexico, where it meant health, luck or fidelity), braided and dry, swaying in an independent cool breeze, cloves pressing up a faint purple under a thin brittle skin.

The first time he saw her move she was just getting up and crossing the road. Independent, graceful, like an animal or something in the air, not in front of anyone, free.

And had it been to talk to someone at the store opposite her stand? It might have been, her aims even now are not known to him.

Life Moves Outside

WHEN I AWOKE in the morning there I heard cries outside, individual, passionate, detached. They entered my sleep as if calling or tapping, calling and tapping, indifferent or sad. Immediately some mundane texture, the sound of an alarm bell, the smell of coffee, entered also. So I located those cries in between being awake and sleeping, such that when I heard them again each morning I felt as though touching a sheet, a sheet familiar and endlessly clean, endlessly washed and waving in the wind, that was connected to the bed I slept on, fitted loosely over my body, naked beneath it. It was what kept me warm, along with the other layers which I perceived, hearing the cries, as being of incalculable weight, the weight of what I woke into.

The word for "here" merges with the word for "now", the word for "there" with that for "earlier" or "later."

The sky was lit up from behind by the sun, which is rising up now in this morning. The ground is a moist and dark place that will dry out by noon and then will again moisten and fall into a semidarkness, into deep red and yellow and orange as the sun sets in the west. So for the morning a pale blue yellow or red (watch and see) maybe even white, for noon bright take dark blue and the golden maple leaves looked up to against it, but leaves not pasted there, the blueness is above, referred to as the vault of space.

That squirrel moving through the green red and yellow leaves, some of which have already fallen and some of which are growing close to the ground, moves in an impervious, cautious, and impulsive way. In front of him golden leaves, suspended from an invisible branch, dance in a silent wind, as I am seeing the whole through glass.

The seam of the ability to move one's glance.

The flowers are orchids, white, in time each one opens. They are sweet, rare, and held on the stem at fixed intervals, determined by the kind of plant.

Telling what moment by moment now amounted to his own story, the former political prisoner is interviewed:

Describe your thoughts in the Ilyushin-62 as you were being flown to an unknown destination.

I had never before flown in an Ilyushin-62, and for that reason alone the flight should have been memorable. But I was in a state of shock from the moment I learned of my release and so for this reason I existed as might a person who has no internal life. I would eat when they served me. I answered questions about the weather posed by the guard who sat alongside me.

As the woman sitting down on the bus straightened her skirt, the child was sure she was about to hear the stranger's story.

"Cold this morning.   Nobody ought to be out of bed this early.   Where are you going?" She paused for a long time between the things she said.

The seat held no holes to retreat into, no doors to close.

"School." That seemed broad and vague.

"Waste of time." And she leaned back, putting her shopping bag down, settling in.

So she wasn't going to tell a story, the girl thought with relief. And the straightening of the skirt had been not the prologue to her narrative but only an assertiveness, an occupation of space in a definite way. She was not the kind, then, who used stories to make herself comfortable.

Mutual facing away appears early on in the pair formation process of gulls, when both partners are not yet fully used to each other and may be seized with an impulse to attack or flee from each other. In these Herring Gulls, facing away or head flagging is an important appeasement ceremony.

The river is full and heavy and flowing. I think about oil when I look at it, though I am sure no oil is in it. Things are so hot they burn the eyes to see, and in water sky condenses as a blue or platinum powder, which is in a liquid form, but thick and shifting.

In "the zone" of a Soviet film, claiming to be science fiction, functioning philosophically and politically, northern creatures occurred in a southern climate.

They travel in flocks and packs and gangs, tracing a figure eight in a brittle geography.

"Something's eating her."

"She's out of her mind with grief."

"O the pain — it's something terrible."

Those sounds you are making have got to be worse than birdcalls, rasping. There is a tone on the phone that sounds like that. It is black plastic and hard. The redeeming light of Vermeer is famous and consoling. How rare it is in this landscape that has always been known for its extraordinary light, but of a different sort — revelatory, blinding, nothing to read a letter by.

The baby, how many days old, lets out a cry. The baby is beginning to look around while in her mother's arms, to not just be still there like a doll or toy, like a thing collapsed in on itself, feeling so intensely, core of flower, its own nature, its own body (all the internal movements rippling over the face and passing in a spasm or stiffness through the tiny perfect body of the newborn) but perching on the mother's arm, post of joy and safety, looking all about. The baby is told the name of her city and her county and her state and her country.

The window is open, sunlight is bright on the keys that wear letters as if they were hats. Suddenly the number, dollar, percentage signs and ampersand take on a peaceful existence there. There is one red key, on it the number one, above it an exclamation mark.

Their mood is no longer contagious. As after a close death, the world is empty, free, yet the shapes in sunlight retain their ability to obstruct or to be touched or to dance in slow motion, shadows on an ever-recurring wall. A curious dignity comes about, the beginning bars of a music, chords of things that do not match but lie there next to each other anyway, their very discordance a form of humility.

Memory is involved he said in knowing one's every need is not being actively denied but simply is wanting, as a plant in light, the shoulders of the growing girl cycling down the street in light, or a character trait is wanting. First she wobbled but now she cleanly drives forward, strongly leaning with her machine. Those are pedal pushers and this the fashion of speech, getting up and going to bed the sentence they neatly said being what happens in between.

Full stops. I knew she was trying to tell me something, and I tried to help her through my coaxing expression which in this case had to seem uninterested but not preoccupied, a feat for sailors and for saints.

Illuminating their most beautiful object they find it casts shadows. These shadows they find distracting. The shadows make them lose their sense of what the object is about. For they like to talk about the object, and how can they go on talking if they have lost their sense. They paint the wall black to lessen or erase the shadows.

The basketball players had seven seconds to get their three points to win the game, and, isolated in their intensity, they were emblems, pure, moving on the court.

He spoke of the professional athletes as a different species.

First, there must be a special respiratory organ, the lungs, affording an immense extent of internal surface, covered by a vascular network, through which the blood flows in innumerable minute streamlets, only separated by an extremely thin membrane from the atmospheric air that has been inhaled; secondly, there must be such an arrangement of the circulating system that fresh blood may be continually driven through the lungs and then onward to the general system; and thirdly, there must be provision for the frequent and regular change of air contained in the lungs.

After leaving the family, young ostriches, still in the monochrome brown plumage of immaturity, form small wandering flocks. They are able to travel at speeds of up to sixty miles per hour, but are nevertheless captured, as they run in circles.

LIFE MOVES OUTSIDE

We were repairing the costumes of the dancers. I was searching for holes and tears caused by the stress of the dancers' bodies within the costumes.

Many go fast on the freeway, and many have died; it is accepted that many more will, that conversation will be limited to what and who is inside the car, the "interior" of which may be upholstered with a velour-like fabric or may be coming apart at the seams. The inside of the car has an intensity unmatched by the other environments they dwell in, and they fill it with music but mostly with noise, brought in on waves projected through the air.

It is accepted that vegetation planted by the freeway will be stunted, will grow in a perpetual weather of the freeway's exhaust. The dependence on oil and the vulnerability to its price fluctuations is lamented as weather. That we will quickly move from here to there with nothing on the way is a "fact of life."

Many think these things, but many do not dream of what they think of, but of something held in the hands like jellyfish, inner life raw or yellow. Holding it in shells, in the hands, such naked flesh suddenly experienced, as if photographed or filmed, entirely forgotten, swallowed whole.

They had two-by-fours and half-decayed decorative square logs, like railroad ties but smaller, and all of this stacked as in a lumber yard but in the store feeling more like an archive, under the roof extending into things like the housewares section and he, who had recently worked for a living with the same materials, looked at the stickers that had been placed, little price tags on each piece of wood, and said: "Isn't that funny the way they put those stickers on, like they were cups."

This was a strange situation, to fall in and out of relation, the way a summer umbrella does to the helpfulness of its shade as fall throws the shadows of clouds over and over it, and it sits solidly planted in its aluminum holder. The terror of all this is so dull that it has virtually disappeared: life appears pleasant, and full of pleasures. Not many of them are secret or treasured, it is true, all of them almost are worn, taken out of the closet, valued, possibly counted, certainly displayed.

Median strip and the runners along it. Broad trees, cars swift, relentless. Often it is mentioned that a person behind the wheel acquires the qualities of his or her machine. A person who would not think of challenging someone on foot, who would smile uncertainly and even imagine the other one's name, insists on right of way, forgetting. I skip over you, I throw a rock, shout the rhymes out, the other girls do too. And the adult activities have the counterpoint of remembered children's games, which serve as waiting room, paradigm, playground, stage set, the flower of time.

Brevity like an axe frees them: the prince cuts his way with no difficulty through the briars of stone.

The young trunks of the citrus trees are painted white or wrapped in rags to keep them from burning in the sun.

Her whole family seems to be made up of tortured souls, who have no reason for being tortured. The apparent semblance of a balanced mind, the phrase "peace of mind" which it once seemed meaningful to question, now appears to have fled.

When she first began writing it was an intensification of feeling. It was a setting of the world of her own family into a larger world. This world, this larger one, was vague and amorphous, and had no known history. When she had the opportunity to attend lectures on world civilization, she ditched them. She was too involved in her emotions and her sexuality to see straight, and found a kind of rightness in living in the following of this passion, which she deemed living passionately.

Thousands of pairs of gannets breed on the island, their photographically accurate memory enabling each bird to find its own nest again after leaving to feed.

I would then be. My mouth over his, his over mine. My mouth over his over mine. Against. When we lift up and shake the blanket in making the bed, it settles down this way. When the air is dry in the dark, raising the covers in getting into the bed, sparks fly sudden, small and white.

Those colors are what one calls primary. To ripen in Russian is to turn in color, and we often use color to judge, judiciously, whether a fruit is ripe. Will it taste good, sweet, soft, yielding and at the same time not be over-ripe, be past its peak, gone, soft, spoiled?

When the flock of birds, of geese, lifts off, they seem to agree on this movement, though a few stragglers, in disciplined form even so, join up with the vast main group, a kind of punctuation, or modifying phrase.

Sunlight. Clean air. The sticker said that survival is a basic human right. There is a soundbox that still works inside the stuffed animal, the leopard whose green eyes glow in the dark.

We call that kind of a marble cat's-eye.

The next day they named the place Acaghcemea, *the meaning of which is given as "a pyramidal form of anything which moves, such as an ant hill."*

LIFE MOVES OUTSIDE 59

In the city she had the distinct sensation, while lying in bed at night, that parts of her mind were orbiting round her head, that she could not contain all that had happened to her. She walked next to this extra, partial body of her own experience, trying to recognize it as her own, or to see it as a discrete entity, or to feel some closeness or relation.

She continually turned to him for reassurance that she was "alright."

What does the mind do, does it digest and eat things. Many animals, he said, have no time to think of anything but eating.

Now those birds, whose feathers are stippled grey and white, almost black and white in this shrouded over light coming through a dense cloud of a sky, overcast, these birds are females I suppose and that one with the orange chest must be the male. They are both busy eating. There are two on the feeder and one is waiting.

The birds aren't sure if the sound of the typewriter is safe. They decide not and leave.

He said he felt human privacy to be a small thing against his first felt violation of the privacy of animals while in the far north. They are white to hide them in the snow, simple as that. Or the privacy of the so-called inanimate world, she flattened herself against the wall to watch him enter without being seen. Atomic privacy wrenched too, bumper stickers saying split wood not atoms. Waste of the plants makes the ocean water warm. This true story bores her, for she has heard it before, living as she does in a family, though with her own phone.

Living as you do. You would then be. Your ear here, tying knots in the supposed calm blue (turquoise, mint, shallow) waters of my intent. Conversation like snorkelling may be an easy tourist sport, and that area, roped off for our observation, seemingly not to be spoiled or harvested, is in truth, or as they say, reality, and on closer examination, cleared every morning of those sea plants and animals not thought by the hotels to be pretty, meaning now "pleasing to the eye," though the original sense of the word, on closer investigation, is found to be "tricky," "cunning," "full of wiles."

The bird outside the window on the new bird feeder that clings directly to the glass could not be too shy still I moved slowly and softly to avoid startling her, dull colored and perched erectly without relaxing whether because in the open at the feeder or whether this is the way birds eat I do not know but at each mouthful the bird straightened itself up and consumed with deliberation.

Masturbation before the mirror heightened the silver quality of the mirror, the way the surface seemed to be brushed on over the glass, or behind it.

LIFE MOVES OUTSIDE 61

He remained convinced through the twenties that writing was at its best a primal instinctive thing like love, and he kept trying to get at the primalcy with a whirl of words as if writing were a physical thing like swimming or running and one simply poured on the muscle power.

This typewriter, while certainly bulky, is a good deal lighter than my previous one. You can tell the date of the typewriter by whether it is rounded. If it is rounded chances are it is the older model. If it is almost plump, almost circular, it is the oldest model which we call A. Then the model with the soft curves is B, and the sleek, elliptical model C, and this latest model, with no curves, has the console look.

Probably for ages after the civilization of man commenced, the still waters of ponds and lakes were the only mirrors.

Although he often felt the boredom of life, in an empty Paris, it was by fulfilling his vocation and by hard work that he was so well able gradually to dissolve the loved one in a broader reality that he ended by forgetting his suffering and feeling it only as if it were a disease of the heart.

The leaves of this tree are like broad fronds, but the tree is covered with them, down to the trunk. It resembles slightly the avocado, but clearly has no fruit, and one wonders, from where it stands, if it was planted or is actually a weed. However we leave it standing.

The peacock was brought to Europe by a mighty conqueror, a man who made history. In its natural habitat it is extremely shy, and only in places where the natives hold it sacred does it become more trusting.

Mean people abound. Senses of humor. Knives. Do not break me. The writing has changed fundamentally, from description, lasso, to request, direction, the hand moving out instead of in. Lasso: a long light but strong rope usually of hemp or strips of hide used with a running noose for catching livestock or with or without the noose for picketing grazing animals.

Tristan Tzara: I detest artifice and lies. I detest language which is only an artifice of thought. I detest thought which is a lie of living matter; life moves outside of all hypocrisy, hypothesis; it's a lie that we have accepted as a starting point for the others.

The black crow doesn't know how to settle on the green palm, whose fronds sway, brilliance, violence, sunlight, under his heavy flapping body that wants to set down on a solid thing.

The offset cover of this book reproduces a photo collage by Phillip Galgiani. The text was linotyped in 10 pt. Palatino by Mollohan Typesetting in West Warwick, R. I. Designed and printed on Warren's Olde Style by Rosmarie Waldrop, smyth-sewn by Bay State Bindery in Boston. There are 1200 paperback copies, of which 50 are signed by the author.

BY THE SAME AUTHOR:

Color (Membrane, 1976)
Disappearing Work (The Figures, 1979)
Robinson Crusoe: a New Fiction (Membrane, 1983)
Two Works for Four Voices (Chax Press, 1986)